CW01509335

# HIGH STEAKS MURDER

## HART TIMES COZY MYSTERIES, BOOK 1

EMMA AINSLEY

SUMMER PRESCOTT BOOKS PUBLISHING

# CHAPTER ONE

Carolina Hart swirled the sweet wine around one more time before she pressed the glass to her lips. From her favorite spot near the window, she could see the time on the clock above the massive fireplace mantel. It was ten minutes until eleven o'clock. Ten minutes until closing time.

She set her wineglass down on the polished oak table and looked to her right to gaze at the rugged Rocky Mountains under the silvery moonlight. After fifteen years, the mountains still triggered awe and mystic wonder deep in her soul. Joe Manfredi manned the bar in his namesake club. He shot distressed looks in her direction as the minutes ticked by. Closing time was upon him, and his last customer appeared in no hurry to leave.

What Joe didn't know was that she had every intention of standing up and walking out of her favorite night spot when the clock struck eleven, but not a second before. In the morning, she would be on the road to Sycamore Ridge, New Mexico. The chances of her ever returning to the mountains were slim.

Carolina surveyed the large space. When she first met the man behind the counter ten years before, she could barely make her way across the room. Thick sawdust had covered the floor in his attempt to capture a western theme. The first time they spoke was when she complained of a splinter from the rough-cut wooden bar stool where she sat at an unpainted wire spool table. Back then, Joe mocked her for wandering into the rough-and-tumble tavern, clearly not meant for fine ladies.

"Maybe this place isn't meant for someone like me, and maybe you prefer a different clientele, but I can tell you that every minute you keep this place looking this uninviting to the women who spend money to visit this valley is another minute you're losing money," she had told him with a smile.

As she walked out the door, the former logger hollered at her to come back and tell him what she meant. Six weeks later, Joe's Tavern reopened with a newer, more sophisticated look. Joe Manfredi never failed to raise his whiskey glass to her when she paid him a visit. Since their initial meeting, his business had grown to the most popular nightspot for the over-thirty crowd. Joe had found out that women in their forties had more cash to spend on wine and whiskey than truck drivers coming off the road for a stiff drink before bedding down in their sleeper cabs for the night.

"Have a good one, Joe," Carolina called out at just before the top of the hour. He held his tumbler filled with amber-colored whiskey up in the air and downed the last swig. Carolina smiled a final farewell to Joe and his place, then walked out to the snow-covered sidewalk with her favorite high-heeled boots pointed toward her cold car.

She pulled the boots off as soon as she climbed inside and set the driver's seat back as far as it would go. The boots landed in an open box in the back when she flicked them behind her one at a time. She took the slip-on shoes from the floor next to her and slid her aching feet into them, then shim-mied into the blue jeans she had left on the seat. Her emerald-green sheath dress came off over her head, and she shivered in the fake silk camisole she wore beneath in the moment it took her to slip the University of New Mexico sweatshirt over her head in its place.

Like the boots, the sheath dress went over the seat and into the box. A mailing label had already been affixed to the outside. Tape and a trip to the post office was all it needed before reaching the woman who had purchased the clothing articles from her. The dress and the boots demanded one last hurrah around town before leaving the mountains forever. She ignored the fact that the clothing should be washed before she sent them off but reasoned that if she bought used clothing from a website, the washer would be the first place it would go after she opened the box.

Carolina turned the key in the ignition and pulled the car out of the parking lot behind Joe's. She wrestled with the thought of hitting the Interstate, but the glass of wine and the flurries swirling around her windshield convinced her to pull into the all-night truck stop and park under the lights until the sun peeked over the mountains first thing in the morning like she'd planned.

She leaned her seat back again and pulled the down-filled bedspread from the back. She crammed a sofa pillow against the window and settled down in her seat. A few hours of sleep meant she'd be more alert for driving the following day. Not that she was terribly eager to leave her mountain paradise. She wasn't ready to let it all go, but life and circumstances had a way of creeping into daydreams and twisting destinies around. She had no choice but to leave.

The snow stopped swirling around three in the morning. Carolina slept for an hour at a time, then woke and watched the starry night sky overhead until fatigue overtook her again and her eyes closed for another hour. At five-thirty, she gave up and started the car with the heater on full blast. She pulled in front of the truck stop and opened her car door. Her legs were stiff when she stepped out, and she held tight to the door frame until her body acclimated to standing upright again.

"Long night?" The words came from a man dressed in a cashmere, quarter-zip sweater, and dark blue jeans. He held the door open for her as she walked inside.

"Something like that," Carolina muttered. He nodded to her and headed off for parts unknown. Out of habit, she glanced at his feet. It was easy to tell the locals from the wannabes. Jackson Hole was no longer a town for Wyoming natives and cowboys. The thousand-dollar boots on his feet told her that he was a wealthy businessman enamored with the western lifestyle. She shook her head and walked to the bathroom. After a few splashes of water on her face, she stood in front of the mirror and took herself in.

Carolina read the truth of her life's circumstances in her reflection. A month ago, she would have never expected to see herself like she was, a plain woman who more resembled the kitchen help than someone fit for the arm of the man who held the door open for her. But it was the truth. She looked more like the small-town twentysomething who had arrived in the mountains with big dreams and a marketing degree than the sophisticated marketing exec, who years later, was on everyone's wish list.

But time passes, trends change, and a pink slip brought the truth home to her. Jackson Hole had outgrown anything Carolina Hart could do for it. Joe's Tavern aside, most of her talents were wasted on the new breed of businesses. She just didn't have it in her anymore, her boss had said when he let her go. He encouraged her to find a small, struggling town back home where her talents could be put to the best use. Her glamorous career, the one her family back home in Sycamore Ridge bragged about at their hometown family restaurant, was gone in an instant.

Add to that the letter Carolina had received a week ago from her beloved Uncle Toad, she made the only decision she felt like she could. She was going home to the same small town she had escaped as a younger woman following her hasty marriage to Billy Sanchez, her high school sweetheart, and their subsequent divorce.

Carolina left the truck stop bathroom and headed straight for the small restaurant attached to it. Her plan was to eat a hearty breakfast, drink a gallon of coffee, then hit the road and drive as long as she could, until she was too tired to see. If she made it home in a day, she would consider herself lucky.

"What'll it be?" Carolina smiled up at the grizzled waiter behind the counter and plucked a menu from the stand in front of her. She scanned the breakfast choices and quickly settled on something.

"I'll start with coffee and the breakfast sampler," she said. "Eggs over hard, bacon and hashbrowns extra crisp, and a short stack. Thanks."

The waiter mumbled something and headed back to the kitchen with her order. Five minutes later, she stared at the plate of food in front of her and prayed that the bacon was better than the coffee. She pushed the eggs around on her plate and thought of the meals she grew up with back home.

Uncle Toad could run circles around the breakfast she had just eaten. When she had her fill, she plopped a twenty-dollar bill down next to her plate and headed back out into the cold. She started her car and turned the heat up all the way, then hit the highway with memories of her childhood growing up in the Hart Family Restaurant swirling all around her.

After a long day of driving and one night in a sketchy motel off the highway, Carolina pulled down the familiar street in the middle of Sycamore Ridge, New Mexico. She waved at Mr. Lopez, owner of Sycamore Ridge Variety, the same five and dime where she had shopped for school supplies and bottles of soda as a child. The store hadn't changed, and neither had Mr. Lopez, aside from a few strands of silver running through his thick, black hair.

Carolina turned into the parking lot of the Hart Family Restaurant and parked next to the green dumpster by the back door. She brushed the wrinkles out of her clothes and quietly let herself inside. Instantly, the smells of home came rushing back to her. She heard the familiar click of the utensils and the din of voices in the dining room. Somewhere in front of the grill, she could hear Uncle Toad's deep belly laugh.

Carolina paused and smiled. Maybe coming home wasn't the worst thing in the world.

# CHAPTER TWO

"Carolina Maria Hart," a familiar voice called out. She beamed at the sight of her Uncle Toad. Although his wispy white hair was a little thinner than the last time she had seen him, he looked great. He held his arms out and swept her up into a tight hug.

"Uncle Toad," she whispered. Fresh tears filled her eyes.

"Are you here to stay?" her uncle asked. He held her at arm's length and smiled when she told him the vague news that she'd be in town for a while after some changes at her marketing firm. "Your parents would be so proud to see you here, home to help out the family business." He shook his head and released her arms. Carolina thought she saw him whisk a tear away from his eyes before he turned back to the grill.

Carolina focused on the inside of the restaurant, trying to think of anything but her parents. She smiled at the never-changing interior of the Hart Family Restaurant. Braided red pepper wreaths were displayed on almost every wall, and copper lanterns lined the long windowsills. She summed it up best when she first arrived in Jackson Hole fifteen years ago. The aesthetic was a cross between southwestern chic and rustic farmhouse. Both represented her parents. Her mother's Mexican tradition was evident next to her father's hardscrabble southern roots. The menu was no different. His mother's southern biscuits and gravy recipe was served right along with a fresh Mexican cuisine.

"Carolina! Are you back for good?" She turned to see another smiling face headed straight for her.

"Marissa?" She stared into the now-adult face of her younger cousin and nodded her head. "Look at how grown up you are!"

"Thank you for not saying how big I've gotten," she said, rubbing her protruding stomach with her hands.

"Oh, Marissa," Carolina exclaimed. "How wonderful."

She nodded. "Due in a month."

"Oh, my gosh," Carolina said after a long

moment. She stepped forward and wrapped her arms around Marissa the best she could.

"You can say it," Marissa said after a minute. "I look like a penguin."

"You look radiant," Carolina said. "I just can't believe you're going to be a mom."

"Neither can my husband," Marissa said. "We tried for five years and then, well, you see the results."

"Well, I'm so happy for you and Danny," Carolina said. She ignored the lump in her throat. "But why are you working here? Why aren't you at home with your feet up?"

Marissa shrugged. "Because I want my son to have this place to start his first job, or maybe even take over some day, and we can't afford to pay outside help anymore," she whispered.

"Are things really that bad?" Carolina asked.

Marissa nodded. "Uncle Toad won't tell you, but yes, things are really that bad."

"He's the one who wrote to me and asked me to come home," Carolina said.

"Did he tell you it's because all he ever talks about is how your marketing superpowers are going to save the family legacy?"

Carolina shook her head. "No, he just said that

he's getting up there in years and wanted to see me before he's too old to know who I am," she said.

"Well, that's what he tells everyone else," Marissa said. She led Carolina to the far side of the dining room and motioned for her to take a seat. "He thinks you're a genius and tells everyone you're going to swoop in and save the Hart Family Restaurant for the next generation."

"No pressure there," Carolina said.

"That's why you're home, though, isn't it?" Marissa asked. "Please tell me you're here to at least try."

Carolina thought back to her last night in Jackson Hole and the pink slip still hidden in the bottom of her suitcase. "Sure." She nodded with a smile. "I'm here to save the Hart Family Restaurant for the next generation."

## CHAPTER THREE

After a few more minutes with Marissa and Uncle Toad, Carolina left to check into a small motel up the road. Just like the restaurant, the Sycamore Ridge Inn still occupied the same century-old building it had since its opening in the 1960s, well before Carolina was born. Like most of the businesses on Main Street, the Sycamore Ridge Inn had not done much in the way of remodeling through the years.

She set her bags down the moment she got into her room and then started a hot shower. She placed clean clothes on the pale-yellow countertop and pulled her long black hair from the clip on top of her head, letting the hair fall around her shoulders. Stepping closer to the mirror, Carolina examined the strands of gray beginning to populate her tresses. She groaned and moved away from the mirror.

A good hot shower was what she needed to clear her head. She stayed under the stream until the hot water began to wane. She dressed and wrapped her head in a towel before leaving the bathroom and settling into the drab motel room. The beige-toned décor stood out in her mind against the swanky rooms she was used to seeing in Jackson Hole.

Everything was different in Sycamore Ridge. Carolina sat down on the edge of the bed. Maybe her dismissal from the marketing firm back in Wyoming was inevitable. Her time was finished. After her fortieth birthday several months prior, she had noticed an influx of young talent. In fact, she noticed younger people in a way she never had before.

Sitting there on the edge of the queen-size bed in the motel room, Carolina considered the fact that she might have aged out of everything in her life she had counted on or taken for granted. She laid back and stared up at the yellow-tinted ceiling, a remnant of the years when smoking was allowed in the motel. Her brief visit to the restaurant told her that her home-coming was a good thing for the rest of her family. Despite the fact that her parents had started the business long before she was born, through the years, everyone in the family had pitched in to keep it going.

After her parents were killed in a car accident when she was just nineteen, her mother's brother Tomas, known to everyone as Uncle Toad, stepped into the driver's seat both as manager of the business and as her parental figure. Carolina loved him ferociously.

She stood up and let the towel fall off her head, then pulled a brush through her hair. For years, Carolina had worn her hair over her shoulders. Thanks to her father's family genetics, her long, black hair dried in ringlets. Back home in Sycamore Ridge, securing her hair in a braid over one shoulder felt like the most natural thing in the world. She didn't need to be fancy or impress anyone like she'd been trying so hard to do the last several years of her life.

An hour after her shower, she felt the walls of her small motel room closing in on her. Carolina placed her cell phone in her designer bag, the only one she allowed herself to keep, and picked up the box with the boots and the sheath dress, planning to head to the post office at the end of the block.

"As I live and breathe," a voice called behind her when she stepped up to the next clerk. "Carolina Hart.

Are you back in Sycamore Ridge to take over your rightful spot as owner of the restaurant?"

She turned around at the question and met the smiling eyes of Gary Martinez, her high school guidance counselor. "Mr. Martinez! It's good to see you," she said. She handed the clerk her debit card and turned back to him. "How are you? Have you retired from the education world?"

"Oh, yes," he said. "Although you shouldn't really call me Mr. Martinez any longer. It's actually Mayor Martinez now."

"You're the mayor," Carolina gasped. "I had no idea you were into politics."

"Well, don't tell anyone, but I'm still not into politics," he said. "I ran because there was a bond issue with the school district, and I fully believed in the need to pass it and improve the schools. That was two terms ago."

"That's amazing," Carolina said. "It was really good to see you."

"It's wonderful to see you, and I'm sure Toad feels the same. You're here in the nick of time."

Carolina thanked the clerk and took her receipt for the box, then turned back to Mayor Martinez. "What exactly do you mean by that?"

The mayor sighed and looked around before he

answered. "I mean that your parents had the right vision for this town when they started Hart Family Restaurant, but there are a lot of new people here developing businesses on the east side of town. Maybe I'm an educator and not a businessman, but even I can see that their flash-in-the-pan business model will not work in a small town like this."

"People sure are expecting quite a bit from me," Carolina said, falling right back into being just as comfortable speaking to him about her feelings now as she had back when he was her guidance counselor.

"Maybe so, but I think you should give yourself credit. You're excellent at what you do, I'm sure of it."

Carolina shrugged. She appreciated the kind words but had no idea what she could do to control what other businesses were doing on the other side of town. "Thanks. I promise I'll do what I can to help."

# CHAPTER FOUR

Early the next morning, Carolina headed into the restaurant for breakfast. She ate quickly and then returned to the back, where Uncle Toad was already slinging hash at the speed of light. With a quick smile, she donned an apron and began to work alongside Marissa during the breakfast rush.

"I'm surprised to see you in here," Marissa admitted when the rush died down.

"Why are you surprised?"

"I don't know," Marissa said. "Just because you have this swanky job in Jackson Hole. It almost seems like waiting tables is beneath you."

Carolina shook her head. "I've never lived under the notion that the place my parents started was beneath me," she said.

"Oh, I don't mean that you feel that way," Marissa said quickly. "I mean that you've earned your way out of an apron. Look at you! You're a college-educated, professional woman. It seems so strange to see you running around filling coffee cups."

Carolina opened her mouth to say more but stopped when she saw the mayor walk up to the front door. He held the door open for a tall, thin woman in a red pantsuit. Blonde hair cascaded over her shoulders and her high heels clicked on the tile floor when she walked inside. For a moment, Carolina thought she was back in Jackson Hole watching a celebrity checking out a local eatery.

Two people followed her inside. A younger man dressed almost as smartly as the lady in red, held his head high when he walked in. Carolina wasn't sure whether she had imagined it, but she thought the woman and the man both held their noses up a little too high when they came inside. The third person was dressed a bit more appropriately for breakfast in the local family restaurant. She smiled in Carolina's direction when she pulled out a seat and sat down.

"Good morning, Mayor," Marissa said brightly when she stepped up to the table to begin their order.

"I suppose you only stock domestic coffee in a

place like this," the woman in red said before the mayor could return Marissa's greeting.

"A local roastery supplies our coffee, yes," Marissa said. "Can I offer you a cup?"

"It will have to do," the woman replied. "But you better have real cream to go along with it."

Carolina felt the heat rise in her neck. She grabbed four white ceramic coffee mugs and a fresh pot and headed to the table. Without a word, she set a mug down in front of the blonde and began to pour.

"Ah, Carolina," Mayor Martinez said. "I would like you to meet Jocelyn Hendricks, owner of Nouvelle Chic Catering. Jocelyn, Carolina's family owns this lovely establishment."

"Charming." Jocelyn sniffed. "How about you bring me some fresh cream for my coffee, Carla?"

"It's Carolina," Marissa corrected.

"Just run along and get Miss Hendricks what she asked for," the young man said. He brushed the air with his fingers as he spoke.

"Who else do we have here?" Carolina asked, ignoring the man. "I'd love to meet all of you."

"Oh, I'm sorry," the mayor said. "This is Paul Wayver and Esme Feldman, Jocelyn's assistants."

"Executive assistant and regular assistant," Paul

corrected. "Now, can we please have that cream, Carla?"

Carolina glared at the man. She wanted to point out that his skinny jeans were not attractive on his pudgy frame but smiled instead. A second later, she placed fresh cream on the table and waited while Marissa took their breakfast orders.

As she expected, the insults and demeaning language did not stop with coffee. Jocelyn began by asking whether the cook was capable of making her an egg white and spinach omelet. She demanded to know where the eggs came from and wrinkled her nose when Marissa explained that they were raised by a local farmer. The line was crossed shortly after when Jocelyn raised her well-manicured hand high above her head and snapped her fingers to get Marissa's attention.

"I'll take over, Riss," Carolina said. She pulled the coffee pot out of her cousin's hands and headed straight for the table.

"Thank you, Carolina," the mayor said as she filled their coffee mugs. She didn't go far when she heard him begin speaking to Jocelyn. "I'm afraid that we're unable to renegotiate the terms of the catering contract for the community awards banquet. As it stands, our budget is limited by yearly donations from local businesses. You're asking me to almost double the price you quoted in the first place, and the original contract was already at the top end of our budget."

"Things have changed a bit since then," Paul interjected.

"In what way has anything changed?" Mayor Martinez asked. "We haven't added to the menu or the number of plates."

"No, but in the three months since we signed that contract with the city, our firm has put another caterer completely out of business in this county," Jocelyn said. "In other words, there is no other competition. Either you renegotiate the contract with me, or you can fend for yourselves. Who knows, maybe the Greasy Spoon here can throw something together and serve it on paper plates."

"Miss Hendricks, that is quite enough," the mayor said. "Your shady business practices aside, I will thank you not to insult our hosts this morning."

"Our hosts?" Jocelyn sneered and shook her head. "You bring me to this hole-in-the-wall diner for a business meeting, and you expect me to act like we're in the middle of some five-star restaurant, Mr. Martinez."

"Mayor Martinez," Esme whispered. "His title is *Mayor*."

"Shut up, Esme," Paul hissed.

"Yes, shut up, Esme," Jocelyn echoed. "I swear, you're worse than my ex sometimes." She shook her head and turned back to the mayor. "You insulted me when you asked for me to 'tweak' my menu to meet the tastes of the townspeople, and you outright disgraced me when you invited me here for a breakfast meeting. But the funny part is that you have no other choice than to go with my contract changes. It's either that or you can figure out how to feed two hundred people in less than a week. I would say the choice is yours, *Mayor*."

By now, all eyes were on their table. Even Uncle Toad and Carolina's second cousin, Noah, emerged from the back to witness her tirade. Jocelyn sat back in her seat and folded her arms over her slight frame. Her smug grin sent an ache through Carolina. Her hands itched to smack it off her face.

Mayor Martinez narrowed his eyes at her, then looked around the room. With everyone watching, he lowered his head in defeat. "I suppose you have me over a barrel," he said. "I don't know how we're going to afford the new contract, but we can't cancel the awards dinner. It's a tradition as old as Sycamore Ridge itself."

"Oh, and you're going to let us fully redesign the

menu, too," Paul added. "It's high time the people in this town got a taste of real culinary excellence." He cast a disparaging look around the room.

"Absolutely not. We already have the menu worked out, and we gave you as much creative space as we were willing." The mayor stiffened. "I can't have you serving dishes most of the people in this town have never heard of. What's the point of that when the dinner is for the community?"

"Then maybe you can just grab a bucket of hog slop from the farm where these eggs come from and throw it out in the middle of the room," Jocelyn shouted. "Because I think I agree with my assistant. It's my way or the highway."

"The highway would be a better choice," Carolina cut in. She stepped in front of the table and faced the mayor. The words tumbled out of her mouth before she could think about what she was saying. "We'll do it, Mayor Martinez."

"You'll do what?" Jocelyn asked. She grabbed Carolina by the arm.

"We will cater the dinner," Carolina said, pulling her arm away. "We'll even do it for ten percent less than the original contract you had with these people." She could hear Marissa's sharp intake of breath behind her.

"You will?" The mayor beamed. "I didn't know you were offering catering services now."

"It's a new business model my beautiful niece came up with," Uncle Toad stepped forward to say. "Our family is working to change things up a bit around here. We can provide you with anything you need, Mayor."

"There is no way you can get away with this," Jocelyn said. "We have a contract."

"Which you technically breached when you decided to push for your one-sided renegotiation," the mayor said. "I'll ask the city's attorney, but I'm fairly certain that move of yours deems the original terms null and void."

"I don't think so. You will honor this contract, and I'll make sure of it," Paul said abruptly.

Esme moved in her chair. "I don't know. Maybe it's a good idea to let these people take over," she said with a wave of her hand. "We can find much better clients who will appreciate us."

"Nonsense," Paul muttered to Esme. "You stay out of this. You should want all the work you can get so you can pay for that oversized house of yours."

Carolina felt her heart thumping hard in her chest. Her hands shook as she spoke. "You heard my uncle," she said, ignoring the arguing fools in front of her.

"We've moved into the catering business, and the city will be our first clients. Hart Family Restaurant has served some of these families for decades, and now we will serve the entire town on Saturday night."

"That sounds like a pathetic marketing slogan," Paul said, wrinkling up his nose.

"It should." Uncle Toad smirked. "Carolina here is a marketing genius from Jackson Hole, Wyoming. She has million-dollar clients and a fancy condo to boot. She's here to help us, and that's just what she's done."

"Well, that's unexpected," Jocelyn said. "By the looks of her, I would have suspected something much different." Her eyes moved up and down Carolina's body as she spoke.

"I think that's quite enough from you, Miss Hendricks," Mayor Martinez said. "It seems we're no longer in business together. I would like to invite you to leave this meeting, so I can speak to my caterer about the menu for this weekend."

Jocelyn cast a disparaging look directly at her. She raised her finger and shook it in Carolina's face. "You have just started a war, lady." She ordered Esme to get her things and then shoved her chair roughly under the table and headed back out the door. Paul stood up and scoffed loudly before he followed her.

Esme stood, carrying everything they'd left behind, and walked out after them silently.

"That was great," Marissa said, clapping her hands in front of her chest. "You were on fire, Carolina! I had never thought to offer catering services, but I can totally see your vision."

"Your cousin is right, Carolina Maria," Uncle Toad said. His eyes misted as he spoke. "You have just breathed new life into this place. I can feel it in my bones."

Carolina allowed herself to be hugged. She returned their smiles and shook hands with the regulars, who left their seats to congratulate her on the new business. Deep inside, her heart raced, and her stomach filled with butterflies. She had spoken in haste, a reaction in anger and disgust to the vile woman who insulted her family and her hometown. Now the reality was beginning to settle in on her.

She had absolutely no idea how she was going to pull off a catering gig with no experience and no business plan for two hundred souls in under six days.

She also had to figure out a way to explain to everyone that she no longer had million-dollar clients or a fancy condo. All she had was herself and, apparently, a new catering business.

# CHAPTER FIVE

Carolina excused herself to the restroom, desperately needing to compose herself. Had she really just allowed that snarky blonde to goad her into starting a catering company out of her family's restaurant? She stared at herself in the mirror. Two hundred people. Six days. And the mayor waiting outside at his table with the details.

Suddenly, everything was riding on her words, words she had spoken in anger. What had she done? Whatever it was, she had to leave the restroom and go face it. Carolina smoothed her hair back into place and turned to open the door.

"Carolina." Mayor Martinez beamed at her when she emerged. "I have to rush to another meeting, but I want to give you a list of the guests and a copy of the agenda. Here's a sample of the current menu, although I have an idea that the menu you're envisioning will look a whole lot different. If you think of any changes, please feel free to make them at your discretion. I trust you and your family."

She accepted the paperwork and thanked him for his time as they walked to the door. "I'll look over the menu right away and get back to you with any changes by the end of the day," she said. Her words came out a little faster than her brain could work. Even if he'd said she could make changes on her own, she wasn't quite ready for that. His approval would make her feel much better.

"I look forward to it, Carolina." He turned to her Uncle Toad. "You know what? All of a sudden, my stomach pains seem to have gone away. I haven't been this excited for years."

"We're glad to hear it, Mayor," Toad called after him.

Carolina's face ached from the smile she'd plastered on. She untied her apron and headed back to the small office that doubled as the storage room. She set the papers down on the desk and practically collapsed in the chair. As soon as her weight hit it, something snapped, and the chair tipped backward. She rolled out and wound up on the floor.

"That chair is broken," a voice called from behind.

Carolina pulled herself up by the edge of the desk and turned around. "Oh, really? I hadn't noticed."

"Glad I could help." He smirked. "Your uncle should have warned you."

"Who are you?" she asked the man standing behind her, holding a tray of biscuits in his arms. She tried reading his age by the lines on his face. His hair was gathered in a low ponytail at the base of his neck.

"Levi Miller," he said. "I work with Toad in the kitchen."

"Well, you seem to know who I am," Carolina said. She wasn't sure why her heart continued to race in her chest. She chalked it up to embarrassment because the alternative wasn't an option.

"I sure do," Levi said. "I also know you're completely overwhelmed, although I have to say that was one heck of a performance out there. I can't think of a better woman to wipe the floor with, either. That Jocelyn woman has had it coming for years."

"I'm sure I don't know what you're talking about." She searched the room for another seat.

"There's a stool on the other side of the freezer,"

Levi said. "I'd get it for you myself, but as you can see, my hands are full."

"Thanks," Carolina said. She walked around him and spotted the stool. "Do you need something?"

"Me? No, ma'am." Levi grinned. "I don't need a thing, but you do. Don't worry, your secret is safe with me."

"What secret is that?" Carolina asked. Her worry and concern were quickly shifting to agitation.

"That you have no idea what you're doing," he said quietly. "Which might be fine, but now you have the hopes and dreams of everyone in this place riding on the words that flew out of your mouth a few minutes ago. You've bitten off a lot, haven't you?"

Carolina studied his face and tried to form an answer in her mind. Before she could open her mouth, Levi leaned in closer. "Don't worry," he said. "If you need help, I'll be here for you. We've got this."

He didn't wait for her reaction before he headed out of the storage room and left her to her own thoughts. Carolina shook her head and took a seat on the stool. She spread the papers out on the desk and scanned the agenda before closing her eyes for a moment. The awards ceremony would take place over dinner. Dessert would be served after the mayor's address and the final award given out for the Sycamore Ridge Person of the Year.

Salads and appetizers, entrees, and finally, dessert. The last part was easy. All she had to do was make and decorate a sheet cake, celebrating the ceremony. She looked over the proposed menu. Her first course included three choices of charcuterie boards, smoked salmon stuffed crepes, or fresh sushi on toasted bruschetta.

Carolina groaned. "Don't try to reinvent the wheel," she said aloud. No wonder Mayor Martinez was excited about them taking over the menu. She would simply give her hometown a taste of what they loved the most about her family's restaurant.

She scanned the rest of the menu, not for any ideas this time, but simply for numbers. She had never planned dinner for two hundred people before, but she had for twenty. Carolina searched the desk for a pen and paper and began to jot down her ideas.

"How's it going?" Marissa poked her head into the office a little while later. She headed for the shelves in the back. "We're out of napkins up front."

"I figured as much." Carolina chuckled. "It's going okay, but I have a lot of planning to do in a short amount of time."

"Well, if you need extra help, you know you can

count on me," Marissa said. "I can get more help, too. If you need it, I mean."

"More help?" Carolina asked.

"Yeah, you know, a catering staff," Marissa said. "I have three friends who would love the chance to make a little extra money right now."

Carolina forced another smile. "Okay, awesome," she said. Personnel wasn't something she had considered yet. "I don't know what an appropriate pay scale is, but let them know that we're hiring."

"Deal," Marissa said. "A few dollars above minimum plus tips should be good."

Carolina nodded. "Sounds good to me," she said. "Let me know their names, and we'll go from there."

Levi returned a few minutes later. "Sounds like your plan is coming together," he said quietly. "You might want to talk to your uncle pretty soon about who's going to cook all of this food you're planning to serve."

"You don't think Toad will do it?" Carolina asked. Her knees weakened a bit at the suggestion that he might not.

Levi shrugged. "I would think the first thing you ought to do is check in with him," he said. "Two hundred people. Man, that's a tall order for one person."

"He'll need help," Carolina said, thinking out loud.

"Which he has, but you still need to ask." He nodded his head at her and left again. Carolina wondered why he seemed to love insisting on reminding her how helpless she was.

.

# CHAPTER SIX

Carolina steeled her nerves and headed into the kitchen. Uncle Toad stood at the grill, still busy, but not in the middle of a rush. She watched as he expertly tossed chopped steak around with diced green peppers and onions. He added a small dish of green chiles and turned the entire mixture upside down into a soft tortilla and added a handful of shredded cheese, then folded the tortilla over and grilled it on all sides.

"Order up," he called out as he plated the food. He checked the next order slip and began a fresh Denver omelet. "Hey, there." He smiled at his niece.

"Hey, Uncle Toad," Carolina said. "I know you're busy, but I was wondering if you might be up for helping me out with the food for the community awards dinner. We haven't really had a chance to talk about all of this. Everything sort of came up all at once."

"Sure, I'm up for helping out," he said. "I hoped you would ask me for my input on the menu, too. I know it all happened fast, but I'm sure you have some sort of plan for this cooked up already. Are we going to call the catering business something different?"

Carolina shook her head. "For now, I think it's a good idea to keep our name since it's already known." That much she knew. Name recognition was as good as money in the bank from a marketing perspective. "If this all goes well, maybe we can call it something like From the Hart Catering."

"I hope it goes well, because that's a fantastic name."

She blushed at his praises. "We can start by adding catering services to the menu and make up some flyers outlining everything. If we can get an endorsement from the mayor after Saturday, that would be even better."

Toad nodded. "Once this thing gets off the ground, we'll make it official."

Carolina wondered if she had it in her to make it work once, never mind several times. "Thanks. I'm really glad to know you're on board with all of this."

"Of course I am." Toad dropped a serving of home fries onto a plate and turned to her. "Hey, do you have any idea where to get ahold of dinnerware and place settings for two hundred people?"

Carolina blanched. Her mind thought up a million ways she could answer, beginning with the confession that she had only just invented the idea of adding catering services to spite the snooty blonde mocking the place. Of all the ideas swirling around in her head, nothing was right. She opened her mouth to tell her uncle the truth.

"Oh, I have a few ideas for that myself," Levi cut in suddenly. "We were just discussing that in the back, anyway. Right, Boss Lady?"

"Boss Lady?" Carolina questioned. Levi narrowed his eyes at her and nodded his head, encouraging her to back him up. "Oh, yes. We're already working on our suppliers."

Toad's face split into a wide grin. "You're helping out, Levi? Man, that's awesome. I could use you in the kitchen with me. Maybe we can do this together."

"Sounds great," Levi said. He gave Carolina a long look and headed back to his station at the prep table.

Toad plated the omelet and turned back to Carolina. "Why don't you put together your ideas, and we can go over everything after the lunch rush? We have another staff member coming in to help. I heard Marissa and her friends are interested, too, but I think we need to chat with everyone at the same time so you can share your vision for the future, Carolina Maria." He took a red handkerchief out of his pocket and wiped his face.

"Sure thing, Uncle Toad," she said. He pulled her into a deep hug and turned back to the grill. "I've got my things spread out on the desk for now. I hope that's okay."

"It's more than okay. I wouldn't mind if you took up all the space in this whole building."

"Where are you staying, by the way?" Marissa asked when she reentered the kitchen.

"Over at the Sycamore Ridge Inn," Carolina said. She had paid for two nights. After that, she had no idea where she might be sleeping. The floor of the office was starting to appeal to her.

"Well, since you're going to be sticking around for a while, there's a trailer over by Danny's folks for sale. It's less than five minutes from here and comes with chickens."

"Chickens?" Carolina asked.

"Yeah." Marissa shrugged. "Whoever left the place had a half acre of land and a chicken coop.

Danny's dad said the place is for sale. If you're interested, I can speak to them for you. I think they bought the land from the bank or something."

"A trailer? Are you talking about that old Airstream just outside of town?" Uncle Toad piped up. "You can't expect someone like Carolina to settle for that. She's used to condos with marble bathtubs and granite countertops."

"You know what? A trailer on a half acre sounds divine, Marissa. And practical. Maybe there's no marble or granite inside, but starting a business requires sacrifice. I'm just looking for somewhere to lay my head at night. How much are they asking?"

"I'll text Danny right now to find out," Marissa said excitedly.

"I'll be in the office."

"You might as well just start calling it your office," Uncle Toad hollered after her. "None of us use it for much."

"I'll be in my office," Carolina called back over her shoulder. She closed the door and sank down on the stool.

"We really need to get you a more comfortable chair for that desk," Levi said from behind her.

"How are you in here again?" She was already doubting the office and the storage room being combined. Working in peace was important some-times, and she couldn't very well have Levi popping up every five minutes if she expected to get anything done.

He stood behind her, filling a large metal bowl with fresh peppers from the small cooler. "Sorry to tell you, but since I'm the prep cook, I spend a lot of time running back and forth between here and the kitchen. I was serious about that chair." He pushed the broken top of the other one out of the way with his feet.

"If you can score a comfortable office chair, I will forever be in your debt," she said. She looked up and stared at him. "Why did you help me back there?"

"Help you? I wasn't helping you, Cinderella."

"Cinderella?" She looked at him sideways, not sure where he was going with his comment.

"Yeah, except you're the version who already has the glass slipper on her foot but has no idea that she holds the keys to the kingdom," he said.

"I can't even begin to pretend I know what that means," she said, staring at him and waiting for him to put his foot in his mouth even further.

He set the large bowl down on the desk and leaned closer to her. "You're here for whatever reason you want to tell everyone else, but I have a feeling there's more to your story than Hometown Girl makes good for herself out in the world and then returns home to save the family business."

"Speaking of business, this is none of yours." The last thing she needed was for one of the restaurant's employees to find out the truth and decide to let it slip to her family that she'd been fired from her job and was no longer of any use in the Jackson Hole marketing scene.

"This whole thing affects Toad and Marissa, and that's why I helped back there. I'm going to continue to help you, too."

"But why? You don't even know me," Carolina said.

"Understand one thing," Levi said, leaning in closer. "My help is not for your benefit. I'm helping you because your help is what your family believes is going to save this place."

"Why does that matter so much to you?" Carolina asked. She was grateful her family had someone looking out for them, but also curious about why he was so adamant about it. She also couldn't tell if she liked Levi or not. He was somehow kind but ominous, and she didn't know how to feel about that.

"Because they matter that much to me," he said.

"You have no idea how lucky you are to have the family you do."

"You have no idea what I do or don't know," Carolina said, immediately feeling the need to defend herself.

"If that was true, you wouldn't have been wasting your time schmoozing rich people in Jackson Hole all these years," Levi said. "You would have been back here acting like the owner of this place and working your fingers to the bone like they have, just to keep this place going."

"You have no right to make that comment," Carolina said. "You definitely don't know enough about me to have decided who I am as a person."

"I know what I owe your family, especially Toad," Levi said. "And I know that I've dedicated my life to making his better."

"What exactly is it that you owe my uncle?"

"That's none of your business." He stood upright and stared at her for a moment, then softened. "If you're here to do right by them, I'll be by your side every step of the way. You won't find a more loyal and hardworking partner than me, but if you're here to take from them because of what you lost somewhere else, I'll do everything in my power to make it as hard for you as I can."

"That's a bold statement." Carolina crossed her arms. "What do you owe my family?" she asked again.

"My life," Levi said. He picked up the bowl and opened the door. "Carolina?" He stopped in the doorway.

"Yeah?"

"I really hope you're the savior your family thinks you are."

## CHAPTER SEVEN

Carolina pulled out another stack of paper and began jotting down menu ideas. Uncle Toad would have his own plans when they met after lunch, but she was determined not to show up empty-handed. Since her parents founded the restaurant, the menu had reflected her mother's roots and her father's deep southern beginnings. It was part of the charm of the Hart Family Restaurant, down-home cooking paired with the best southwestern fare in town.

For the purposes of this dinner, she decided the focus ought to lie more on her mother's side of her heritage. Appetizers were easy. Nachos and queso, fresh chicken tortilla soup, empanadas, and quesadillas. Dessert could be simple, too. She would serve flan and sopapillas with warmed honey.

Her biggest issue was the entrée. She pulled out the information Mayor Martinez had given her again. Buffet style would be so much easier, but she had so much riding on the awards dinner. She scanned the agenda once more. The meeting began promptly at seven. Opening remarks were followed by appetizers, and a few speakers followed. The keynote address would be given by the mayor during dinner, followed by the awards ceremony and dessert. The entire affair was slated to last three hours.

Three hours? Surely the speakers wouldn't talk that long. She studied the list of speakers a little more closely, then turned to the original contract with Jocelyn's company. "Bingo," she said when she spotted the section detailing the timeline for the night. Appetizers served at seven, but dinner didn't start until 8:30. She added up the timing for the speakers, but even with the mayor's half-hour-long speech, there was plenty of time for a buffet.

The packet of information included a layout of the meeting hall where the dinner was set to take place. She turned the diagram around a few times. Twenty round tables were set up in the center of the room with ten people to each table. She studied the outside of the space, the four corners around the room. If she set up stations on each side, it would work out perfectly.

She wrote a list of potential stations, including a taco bar, burrito station, nachos, and sliders. Hamburgers might be from the other side of the menu, but she couldn't think of a better option. She stood up and headed toward the kitchen, smiling with the progress she had already made. Next, she needed to estimate the amount of each ingredient she would need to order and then make the order as soon as possible.

Her uncle already had his apron off when she entered the kitchen, and Levi stood behind the grill ready to take over.

"You want the special?" Uncle Toad asked her.

"Absolutely," she said with a grin. He smiled and began fixing a plate for her.

"Meet you out there," she said. "I need to run to the restroom first." Carolina ducked into the ladies' room and caught her breath when she stepped in front of the sink to wash her hands. It was her reflection in the mirror above the sink that caught her eye. She wore minimal makeup, a far cry from her life in Jackson Hole, but her face was practically glowing. She was smiling, and it surprised her. She hadn't seen her own smile in forever. At least not a real one.

She opened the door and headed out to have lunch with her uncle. She was filled with the warmth of nostalgia and the fierce love she felt for the man who had stepped into her parents' shoes when they passed away. He winked at her when she emerged from the small alcove where the restrooms were situated.

"So, let's talk about catering," he said when she sat down across from him. "Tell me the ideas you have."

Carolina handed over the diagram with the list of stations and waited for his response. "I think you're onto something here, but I think it would be easier to offer just three choices per course."

"Three choices sound doable," she said. "Since you're the cook, why don't you tell me what you think we should do?"

"Well, since this is our first time out, I think we should stick to our strengths," he said. "Our best-selling apps are the empanadas, flautas, and the chicken tortilla soup. The first two share the same dipping sauces so that will simplify it, too."

Carolina smiled. He was definitely making sense. "How about the desserts? You want three choices there as well?"

"The first two you figured out on your own. Flan

and sopapillas are perfect, but to keep with the theme of three choices, let's go with a Tres leches cake."

"I figured we would need a sheet cake for the gathering, anyway," she said.

Uncle Toad shook his head. "Unless the mayor specifically requests it, this is us putting on dinner for them," he said. "They're already getting awards. We're there to feed them better than they have eaten all week."

"Unless they've already been here."

"Yes, unless they have already been here." He chuckled. "Which leads me to the main dishes. I like the idea of stations. In fact, I think a taco bar, a nacho station, and a made-to-order fajita station are the best ideas."

"You want to go with an all-Mexican meal?" Carolina asked.

"Yes, because that's fewer ingredients to order and fewer to prep," he said. "That doesn't mean that the next catering gig won't include a burger station and a taco bar, but for simplicity's sake, I think this is the way to go."

"Uncle Toad, I think you're a genius, and I bow to your expertise," she said.

"Well, it's you who turned your own life upside

down to come home and breathe new life into this old place." He beamed.

Carolina sighed. "About that," she said. "Uncle Toad, there are some things you should know…"

"You have to help me." Jocelyn Hendricks rushed into the dining room and headed straight for Carolina's table. "You need to tell the sheriff I was here earlier! He thinks I killed him!" She plopped down next to Carolina and shoved her over.

"What are you talking about?" Carolina asked, moving over in the booth to make room for Jocelyn.

"I'm talking about the sheriff," Jocelyn shouted at her. "He's on his way over here to ask you about my interaction with him. You have to tell him it wasn't me!"

"Jocelyn, calm yourself down," Uncle Toad halfway stood up and spoke. "Why is the sheriff coming here?"

"Because someone ran Paul off the road after he left here, and the sheriff thinks I did it. He thinks I'm a murderer! You must tell him it wasn't me."

"For one thing, why would I tell the sheriff anything?" Carolina asked. "And for another, why in the world would he believe me? I don't even know who he is."

"Actually Carolina Maria," Uncle Toad said. "You do know him."

Before she could ask him what he meant, the sheriff walked into the restaurant. "Billy," she gasped when he walked in. "You're the sheriff?"

"Hello, wifey poo." Billy smirked. "When did you get back in town?"

# CHAPTER EIGHT

"Please, that's why you have to tell him that it wasn't me who killed Paul," Jocelyn said. "Listen to her, Sheriff. She'll tell you."

"Carolina, are you friends with Jocelyn Hendricks?" Billy asked her.

"I never met this woman before today, and I am not your wife."

"Are you sure about that?" Billy asked her. "Because my divorce papers never showed up."

"Can we please focus on me?" Jocelyn shouted. "I did not touch a hair on my assistant's head, Sheriff."

"Which one?" Billy turned his attention to her and asked. "Seems like both of your assistants are in trouble. One is dead and the other is missing."

"Both of them?" Carolina asked, looking at Jocelyn with wide eyes. "What is going on?"

"If I knew that, I could prove to this neanderthal that I am not guilty of murder," Jocelyn said.

"We found Paul Wayver's cell phone lying on the ground next to his body and his totaled vehicle," another officer said. She stood behind the sheriff. Carolina had not noticed her coming in, but she was hard to miss now. She was stunning.

"So? There's nothing crazy about someone's cell phone being close to their body," Jocelyn said. Carolina wondered if the woman ever stopped to think about what she was about to say before she opened her mouth.

"It's a little crazy when there is a death threat on there from you," Billy said.

"A death threat?" Uncle Toad asked, moving away from Jocelyn.

"Yeah, she wrote that she was going to tie an apron around his neck and hold it there until he turned purple, or his head popped off, whichever came first," the deputy said.

"This is insane," Jocelyn said.

Billy reached behind his back and pulled out a pair of silver handcuffs. "Come on, Ms. Hendricks.

Let's not make any more of a scene than you already have here."

"No, no, no," Jocelyn said. She covered her face and began to cry. "I'm too pretty to go to jail."

"That may be, but you are the only suspect we have at the moment, and the evidence doesn't point in another direction," the deputy said. "Stand up, or I'm going to slap these on you in front of everyone."

"Someone else had to have done it," Jocelyn said. She removed her hands from her face and looked wildly around the room. She glared at Carolina. "You! Maybe it was you. You made all that trouble in here this morning with the mayor! You stole the awards dinner from me."

"If Carolina was going after someone, I don't think it would have been your assistant, Jocelyn," Marissa said, coming over to the table.

"Please, don't try to help me," Carolina whispered.

"She's right, though," Uncle Toad said. "Carolina didn't even know him."

Jocelyn waited until the auburn-haired deputy pulled her out of the booth seat before she would stand up. Carolina looked up in time to see Levi watching everything with curiosity from the pass-through window in the kitchen.

"Call my attorney," Jocelyn shouted on her way out of the building. "I need my lawyer. You owe me, Carolina. You stole my business from me!"

"Umm, you just tried to throw me under the bus as the killer," Carolina mumbled. She shook her head and stared at her uncle. "What the heck is going on right now?"

"Two things," Uncle Toad said. "One, you just found out that you and Billy are still married, and two, you just started an even bigger war with Jocelyn Hendricks."

"Oh, hush. I'm not still married. Billy just likes to mess with me," she said. "I never asked for a war with Jocelyn. I only just met her today."

"It doesn't take much with that woman," Marissa said.

Marissa and her uncle continued to chatter about the arrest while Carolina zoned out to their words. She sat back in her seat and wracked her memory about the details of her divorce fifteen years before. She made numerous trips to her attorney's office, appeared before a judge, and signed papers. That meant she was divorced, right? Billy Sanchez sure had a way of getting into her head and making her second-guess herself and reality.

# CHAPTER NINE

"A man is dead," Carolina said to her uncle and cousin an hour after Jocelyn's arrest. "I can't believe they were all just here this morning, and now that man is dead."

"He was a snobby little man," Marissa said under her breath.

"Marissa," Uncle Toad said sternly. "Do you really think we ought to speak ill of the dead?"

"He wasn't exactly a little man anyway," Levi added.

"Okay, you guys," Uncle Toad said. "He was a very unpleasant and portly man, but he's dead now. That's more disturbing than anything."

"You're probably starting to wonder what you

came home to," Mayor Martinez said. He had arrived a few minutes before to check on her progress with the menu.

"As terrible as I feel about the death of Jocelyn's assistant, and as disturbing as her visit and all of this is, we still have other matters to focus on," Carolina said. She wanted to add how the entire situation really had nothing to do with her, but feared she might sound heartless about the recent death. The truth was, the death, even the murder, of someone she had barely met really had very little to do with her.

"Mayor, we have a working menu," Uncle Toad said. He motioned the mayor into the kitchen. "I hope this works for you."

"Oh, this is such a relief," Mayor Martinez said, looking over the menu. "Don't get me wrong. I have been to events Jocelyn and her team have catered before, but you sort of get there, stand around and look at a handful of food in the middle of a plate and leave again as hungry as when you started out. Your menu looks like a real dinner."

"Really?" Carolina asked. "You're alright with it?" If she didn't know better, she'd have thought that the mayor was almost too happy to have them catering in Jocelyn's place.

Mayor Martinez smiled. "I'm delighted with it," he said. "Besides, it will be so nice not to hear Jocelyn excoriate her staff. She was always yelling at one person or another."

"Did she yell at her assistants in the same way?" Carolina asked. Her curiosity was piqued.

The mayor nodded his head vigorously. "Yes, especially that mousy girl, Esme," he said. "Paul got his share of her anger, of course, but he was basically her mirror image. It's hard to tell what their relationship was, honestly. They were either clashing because they were so much alike, or had their noses held high, thinking they were better than everyone."

"It's possible that she really did murder him, then," Uncle Toad said. "I can't believe that woman."

"Either way, I hope they find out who did this," the mayor said. "Even if the man was technically killed outside of the city limits, it reflects poorly on Sycamore Ridge."

"Mayor, I was just wondering something," Carolina said. "If Jocelyn was so awful, why did people hire her?"

"Because anytime another company was hired, she made sure to do what she could to ruin them and their business. If it didn't go as planned, she'd send her assistants out to make their lives miserable, so eventually, the competition would just give up."

"So, it's possible that someone from one of those companies that she pushed out might have had an unpleasant dealing or two with Paul and been angry enough to kill him?" Carolina asked, trying to think of another person who could have done something so awful. It was almost unbearable for her to consider that the mayor himself may have done something devious in order to get out of doing business with Jocelyn's company.

Mayor Martinez frowned. "I suppose, but that's not what this is about. I'm glad to be rid of her, especially now that Paul is gone. She'd never have been able to run this event without him."

Carolina froze and did her best to hide her curiosity. Two things struck her as odd. The first thing being if Jocelyn couldn't run an event without Paul, there'd be no reason for her to kill him, because it would affect her business. Second, if Mayor Martinez did have something to do with this, it would have ensured that Jocelyn wouldn't have been able to do without Paul, and even if she tried, she'd be terribly busy dealing with that, giving her less time to fight him on the contract.

"Right, uhh, definitely," she said. "Let's not talk

about that for now." She cleared her throat and looked at her uncle.

"So, we're good with the menu, correct?" Uncle Toad nodded expectantly. He appeared to be completely oblivious to what Carolina was thinking.

"Do you have enough personnel to pull an evening like this off?" the mayor asked.

Carolina cast a look at her cousin Marissa, who nodded and smiled in return. "We have enough staff, and like I told you, we will do this for ten percent less than Jocelyn's original estimate."

"That's music to this mayor's ears," he said. "I look forward to Saturday night. If you need early access to the community building, just let me know. Thank you all." He beamed again at Carolina and turned to leave.

"I just can't believe it," Uncle Toad said when the mayor was gone at last. "We're caterers now. I wonder what my sister and brother-in-law would think of this place now?"

Carolina shrugged and smiled at her uncle and then excused herself to the office. Any mention of her parents hit a raw nerve she wasn't ready to confront. Not to mention, this murder was getting to her already. The idea that her sweet, high school guidance counselor could have hurt someone made her sick to her stomach. He seemed thrilled to have his costs cut, but he knew the restaurant was struggling, and Carolina was afraid to believe that he'd planned this out, down to the very last, most morbid detail.

She sat down at the small desk and looked over the proposed menu again, trying to focus. They really didn't have all that much time to get this done, and if she spent what little time she had worrying about Jocelyn, she'd never get anything accomplished. With another blank sheet of paper, Carolina began the process of figuring out what she would need to pull the event off. She wrote down everything she could think of, every potential ingredient, then sat and stared at the list. Now that she knew what to order, she just needed to know how much.

"Let Toad do that part," Levi said over her shoulder a moment later. Carolina jumped on the wooden stool, nearly losing her balance.

"I didn't hear you come in," she said, a bit exasperated. "Maybe you should knock."

"Right," Levi said. "I'll be sure to start knocking on the door to the storage room now, after working here for the past eight years."

"You've been here eight years?" Carolina asked.

"You haven't," Levi replied. "Some owner you are."

"What is your problem?" Carolina snapped. "I might be the technical owner, but Toad took over and manages it way better than I ever could. I don't ask for money, and I don't do anything that makes it seem like I should run this place. My name is on the business because it belonged to my parents. That's it. Are you trying to get me to hand the place over or what?"

"I thought I already explained all of this," Levi huffed. "I see through you. I know your presence here isn't the altruistic act of coming home to save the family business that everyone else thinks it is."

"So, what difference does that make to you?" she asked. "This is still my parents' restaurant and my family, not yours. If you aren't willing to go into details about your closeness with my family, then I don't think you have a right to give me such a hard time."

"Family comes in more than just blood," Levi snapped.

"Okay, you're cautious about me," Carolina said. "Fine. But you barely know me. How do you know I don't plan on achieving great things here?"

"I don't," Levi admitted. "I also don't know how you plan to pull off the things you have promised your family, like this dinner."

"I plan to do it through hard work and sheer determination," Carolina said.

"That's sounds great on a greeting card, but how is that going to pay for the equipment you're going to need? Or the extra money for the food you need to order, on a rush order now, of course," Levi asked.

Carolina inhaled sharply and folded her arms defiantly. "For one thing, I plan to check out the community center this evening just to see where we stand with serving dishes, a warming table, and place settings," she said. "For another, I happen to have a little money saved back from my last position."

"Money you're going to use to buy that rundown trailer Marissa told you about earlier?" Levi asked.

"Maybe I have enough to do both," Carolina said stiffly.

"That's fine, reasonable even, but like I told you before, don't go making promises you can't keep. I will not stand by and watch Toad get hurt."

Carolina felt the indignation crawl to the top of her head. She slid off the stool and faced him. "You know what? I'm getting a little sick of your attitude, Levi," she said. "Who do you think you are?"

"Is something wrong?" Uncle Toad asked from the doorway. He filled the entire frame. For a moment, she could see her mother's face in his.

"Nothing is wrong." Carolina forced a smile. "Except for the fact that this guy doesn't think I know how to cook, and he's giving me grief about it."

Her uncle looked at her sideways. "Do you know how to cook?" he asked her with a grin. "Because I don't remember if you've ever cooked anything edible."

"That's enough." Carolina couldn't help but laugh. She wadded up a piece of paper and threw it at her uncle in retaliation. He dodged the paper missile and chuckled.

"I was just coming to tell you that I will get a final order list to you right after work so we can call the food distributors first thing in the morning and get food ordered for this weekend," he said. "Also, I think we might need to find a van to deliver the food with."

"We also need a way to keep everything warm while it's still here," Levi added. He sent a knowing look in Carolina's direction. "I'm sure the venue has everything else we'll need."

"Oh, you're right," Uncle Toad said. "I hadn't thought of that, but we will need a buffet table here, too. We can't cook everything all at once for two hundred people."

"I will see to that myself," Carolina promised.

"I'll drive up to the city after work and look for an equipment store."

"Don't you have to go with Marissa to her in-laws' place and look at that trailer?" her uncle asked. "Will you have time to do both?"

"I'll make time," Carolina said, smiling reassuringly. "Don't worry, Uncle Toad. I've got this."

## CHAPTER TEN

Carolina followed Marissa out of the Hart Family Restaurant parking lot and down the road after Marissa's shift ended. Her in-laws lived less than five minutes outside of town, but the difference between where they lived and the small town of Sycamore Ridge was startling. Carolina had forgotten how the New Mexican countryside could appear both beautiful and desolate at the same time.

Herman and Margie Lopez lived on ten acres in a beautiful Spanish-style ranch house. Marissa waited with her mother-in-law in the spacious kitchen while Herman showed Carolina the small trailer on the adjacent half-acre lot. Even at dusk, the red desert sun reflected on the shiny exterior of the trailer.

"The previous owner left in a huge hurry,"

Herman said as he showed her inside. "It's not much, but for a single person, this is sufficient." He waited while Carolina walked through the narrow space. She was surprised at the condition of the interior.

"Are there issues with the plumbing or anything?" she asked, peeking in at the small bathroom.

"Nope." Herman shook his head. "The plumbing and electrical have been inspected by professionals. I can show you the paperwork."

"How much are you asking for the trailer and the lot?"

"Ten thousand," Herman said. "The chickens and the coop come with it. Right now, my wife is feeding and looking after them, and she collects the eggs, too."

"How many eggs does she get a day?" Carolina asked.

"About two dozen." Herman beamed. "There's more than thirty chickens in there."

"What am I going to do with thirty something chickens and two dozen eggs a day?" Carolina asked.

"We'll help you eat the eggs," Herman offered. "Or you can take them to your restaurant, I suppose. That's probably not enough to do much, though."

"True." She stepped back outside and looked at

the coop, a converted old shed larger than the trailer itself. "Have you had much interest in this place?"

"Oh, yes," Herman said. "We have a lot of people interested, but I quoted fourteen thousand to them. We would really like for you to have it."

"You would?" Carolina asked. "Why?" They rejoined Margie and Marissa in the kitchen of the larger house.

"You're family to Marissa and our son, Danny," Herman said as he held the door open for her. "It's always better to live next to people you already know."

"We've had issues with other people who have lived here for a short time," Margie answered. "A place left vacant like that for long attracts people. The kind of people we don't want."

"Just last night, we could have sworn we saw someone in the chicken coop," Herman said. "I went and checked it out, and there was no one there, but it is a comfort to know when someone is living there. If you're interested, you would be the best possible person to move in, aside from our own kids."

"Danny and Marissa here need a much bigger place." Margie patted her daughter-in-law's large belly.

"Well, ten thousand is a wonderful deal," Carolina said. "I'll get the money to you tomorrow morning."

"Oh, you're paying in cash?" Herman asked. "We were going to arrange payments if that's what you needed."

"I'm sure Carolina can handle it." Marissa winked.

"I will bring a cashier's check from the bank, if that's okay," Carolina said. She was sorely tempted to ask more about their payment plan options but decided to keep up appearances for Marissa's sake. The property itself was a steal at that price, and she had it in the bank thanks in part to the large severance package she'd received when she was asked to leave the marketing firm.

Several thousand dollars remained in her account, most of which she planned to spend on the equipment to get the supplies they would need for the catering job. She thanked Herman and Margie and promised to return as soon as the bank opened in the morning. Herman handed her the keys and invited her to move her things over from the motel as soon as possible.

Carolina waved at Marissa on her way out of the Lopez's driveway. She calculated the amount of money she would have left in her account as she drove. She wondered if it was going to be enough to see them through to the next job. She might have had enough money to live for a short time, but it was dwindling much faster than she'd expected.

It occurred to her then that she hadn't thought that far into the future, but she had to start thinking about it right away. No doubt she needed equipment. Despite the fact that the restaurant was already a commercial kitchen, it was a smaller kitchen, and the daily operations would still have to continue. She hoped they could keep up with breakfast and lunch during the day and save the catering gigs for the evening.

Carolina's head began to ache as she considered the many things she would need for a catering business to run smoothy and professionally. She had no idea if Jocelyn's company would survive her arrest for murder, or even if Jocelyn had committed murder. According to her insistence, she had not, and according to Carolina's feelings, there was much more to the story. Either way, she would be competition for the Hart's, or the void left behind by her absence would throw them into an upheaval.

Forty-five minutes after she left her new home next door to Herman and Margie, Carolina pulled into the parking lot of Chefs and More, the closest restaurant supply retailer in the area. She parked close to the front under the parking lot lights and headed inside.

Immediately upon walking inside, Carolina felt overwhelmed. She walked to the middle of the store, lost in a sea of stainless-steel pots and pans. The massive store stretched out in all directions.

"Carolina?" a small voice called behind her.

She turned around to face Esme Feldman, the young woman who had been with Jocelyn when they met earlier that day.

"Esme! Where have you been?" Carolina gasped. "Everyone is looking for you."

"Who is everyone?" Esme asked her.

"Jocelyn and the sheriff, for starters," Carolina said, realizing she had no idea if there was a search party out on the woman or not. "The sheriff said you were missing. It's one thing to be missing because something bad happened to you, but it's another thing to take off after someone you work with was killed. Since no one had that answer, I'd say it doesn't look very good on your part."

"Wait," Esme said. She guided Carolina into a small aisle of saucepans. "What do you mean, someone was killed?"

"You don't know?" She studied the look on

Esme's face, trying to decide if she was telling the truth or not.

"No," Esme gasped. "I left right after the meeting with the mayor this morning. I told her I quit and came here."

"Here to the restaurant supply store?" Carolina asked.

"Yes, I work here," Esme said. She touched her blouse, pointing out a name tag Carolina had not noticed. "I've been working here part-time for quite a while now. Jocelyn's hours were so up and down and unpredictable that I had to get a second job. I need to make money somehow, right?"

"What happened after you left the meeting?" Carolina asked. Her curiosity got the better of her. She'd told herself before that she wanted to focus on the catering event, but seeing Esme had her mind reeling in all the worst ways.

"Paul and Jocelyn got into a screaming match in the car on the way back to the office," Esme said. "I had enough, so when we got back, I got out of the car and headed inside long enough to gather my things and tell Jocelyn that I quit. I guess she was too busy yelling at Paul to hear what I said because she didn't even reply to me."

"Why were Paul and Jocelyn yelling?" Carolina asked. From her memory of the meeting that morning, Paul was more apt to agree with Jocelyn on everything.

"They fought all the time over what to serve, uniforms, and the vision for the catering business," Esme said. "Paul told her accepting a job like the awards dinner Saturday night did not convey the image he wanted for the company."

"Why would his image matter? I thought he was Jocelyn's assistant," Carolina said.

"Oh, he is, but he's also an investor in her company. He was supposed to be a silent partner, but that hasn't worked out. They fought all the time over it, so much that Jocelyn's boyfriend broke up with her because he was tired of listening to all the drama. She hated any reminder that Paul had to put his own money into her company, and Paul never wanted to let her forget."

"Well, I guess that's motive enough for murder," Carolina said, thinking not only about Jocelyn but also her ex. "I wonder if the sheriff knows about all of that, too?"

"The sheriff," Esme said nervously. "Why would he need to know?"

"Because he arrested Jocelyn this afternoon for Paul's murder," Carolina said.

Esme shook her head. "This is all too much," she said. "No matter how much they argue, the thought of Jocelyn killing anyone just doesn't make sense to me. It had to be someone else."

"Okay. What are you thinking? Her ex, an old employee, or maybe someone from a rival business? Maybe it wasn't about Paul at all, but instead someone who thought killing him might cause Jocelyn enough problems to make her lose her business?"

Esme looked around the aisle and down at her feet. "I really couldn't say. They've both made lots of people angry over the years. Paul had money, and a lot of it, but he didn't have the people skills Jocelyn does."

Carolina couldn't hold in her laugh. "Jocelyn has people skills? Who knew?"

Esme's lip curled. "Believe it or not, she has a way of getting things done. It might not have always been the best way, but she made things happen."

Carolina thought about Jocelyn's way of making things happen and felt like it was more bullying her way into things than anything else.

"If you think of anything, please give me a call, or stop by the restaurant. I plan to be spending most of my time there. Even though that's where Jocelyn was arrested, it hasn't seemed to slow business down any."

"That's where they arrested her? I'm sure she loved that." Esme smirked.

Carolina nodded. "Yes, and when they took her away, she begged me to help her get in touch with her lawyer. I have no idea how to do that. Do you?"

"I'm rather surprised you want to help her, but you can leave that to me. I know who she uses, and I still have access to pretty much everything. I'll give them a call as soon as I get off work tonight. It's the least I can do."

"After what you just described as your last day working for Jocelyn, that is very nice of you," Carolina said. "Now, if you will excuse me, I have to find a warming table. It seems I just started a catering business."

"You're in luck. I know just where one is, and I can help you find everything else you might need as well. I make a commission," she added quietly as she led the way around the store.

Esme walked her through buying additional cooking and bakeware, plates and bowls of various sizes, flatware, and cups for over two hundred people. Carolina had not planned to buy the tableware just yet, but Esme pointed out that the next catering job might not take place at a facility already equipped with those items.

One hour and an entirely too-high bill later, Carolina was out the door. Esme helped load the car with the things she had purchased. In addition to what she'd gotten at the store, she'd also ordered a buffet table with a temperature-controlled base, set to be delivered to the restaurant in two days.

Carolina still needed to add more to her supplies, but the glassware, wine glasses, and champagne flutes would have to wait for a few more paydays. She hoped the next catering gig she landed was not a wedding. She started a long conversation with herself on the way back to Sycamore Ridge. She desperately needed to find a vehicle large enough to transport the food and equipment. Her own four-door sedan was not going to work for long. She also needed to find space for the additional equipment at the restaurant. There would be no space inside the little trailer she had just bought, and she doubted anyone would want to hire a caterer who used a chicken coop to store her pots and pans.

Carolina needed to speak with Uncle Toad as soon as possible about a game plan, but for now, she had to figure things out on her own. Instead of the Sycamore Ridge Inn, she headed for the Hart Family Restaurant.

At least for tonight, she could unload some of the boxes and leave them inside the storage room.

A light burned inside the building when she pulled into the parking lot. She parked behind the back door, angling her car just a couple of steps from the door for easier transport of the boxes. She grabbed a stack of baking sheets and wrestled with her keys.

"What are you doing here?" Levi appeared in the doorway. His face was flush. Perspiration dripped off his chin and onto his unwashed shirt.

"What are you doing here?" Carolina demanded. "I happen to own this place."

"I was just working," Levi said, a little too quickly. Another person appeared behind him, a large man with a rough-cut face and a scowl to go with it.

"Who is this?" the other man asked.

"She's the owner," Levi said quickly. He looked nervously over his shoulder at the man standing behind him. "We'll have to pick this up later."

"Fine," the other man said. He made his way past Levi, nearly pushing Carolina out of his way as he passed her and left through the back door. A second later, he was on the back of a loud motorcycle she hadn't noticed, heading swiftly out of the parking lot.

"What is going on around here, Levi?" Carolina asked.

"None of your business," he snapped. He ignored her standing in the way of the back door and headed outside.

"We're not finished here," Carolina called out behind him.

"Obviously," Levi said, returning inside. He carried one of the heaviest boxes from her car.

"You're not leaving?"

"Did you want me to leave?" he countered.

"Yes. No," Carolina stammered. "I mean, was that guy some kind of a drug dealer?"

Levi stopped and glared hard at her. "Please tell me you didn't just ask me what I think you did."

"It's a fair question, and you know it." Her voice was a little shakier than she wanted it to be. "He looked the part."

"After where you've been, I'm sure everyone looks the part, Cinderella," Levi said.

"Stop calling me that name," Carolina shouted.

"Stop assuming that I'm some sort of drug dealing ex-con," Levi shouted back as they glared at one another over who was going to carry what box inside.

"I never said I thought you were." Carolina stepped out of the way as Levi moved past her with another heavy load for the storage room.

"No, you just think I hang out with drug dealers in your restaurant after hours," Levi sneered.

"You have to realize how it looks," Carolina said, following behind him with a smaller box.

"I know how many different ways that might have looked," Levi said. "It's clear where your mind goes when it comes to assuming things about people like me."

"Well, you sort of do have the look of a seasoned motorcycle man going on," Carolina said with a grin.

"Yeah? You look like you're more comfortable in high heels and a tiara than jeans and a sweatshirt, but who's judging?"

Carolina looked down at her attire and blushed. "If that guy wasn't up to no good, who was he?"

"A buddy of mine from years back," Levi said. "He has a line on a used panel van. I was trying to work out a good deal with him. I was here in the first place because I was cleaning out the deep fryer before the weekend, so Toad didn't have to mess with it."

"Tell me more about this van," Carolina said. She grabbed the last load from her trunk and slammed it shut.

Levi surprised her with a burst of laughter. "You're unbelievable," he said, shaking his head. "A minute ago, you practically accused me of scoring a drug deal in the kitchen after hours, and now you want to hear all of the good news about the van I want to get for the catering business."

"Okay, I was wrong about the man," Carolina said. "I suppose I might be wrong about you, too, but the jury is still out on that one."

"Likewise," Levi said.

"Can we just forget about this and start over?" Carolina asked. "I'm a little out of my depth with all of this, and you seem to be the only person here who can see that."

"Is that supposed to make me feel sorry for you?"

"No, not at all, but it is supposed to sound sincere and real because it is. I have no idea what I'm doing. You're right about that, but coming back here wasn't just for my family, it was also for myself. I got fired from my fancy job in Jackson Hole, and I don't want my family to know about it, but not because of my pride. It's because of what they assume about me. I can't bear to break their hearts right now."

"Why were you fired?" Levi asked.

"Because the marketing ideas I had fifteen years ago are fifteen-year-old ideas now," she said. "To put it bluntly, I aged out."

"That's harsh," Levi said.

"It wasn't pleasant," Carolina said. "My uncle

wrote me a letter begging me to come home and help the restaurant the same week I got the pink slip."

"And here you are, hoping it was a matter of divine intervention," Levi said.

"I'm hoping that I still have enough left in me not to wreck this business, too," Carolina said quietly.

"What about your husband, the sheriff?" Levi asked. "What's the story there?"

"He's not my husband," Carolina said. "At least, not now. I divorced him when I was twenty-four and headed out of town as fast as I could afterward. Why are you asking me about Billy?"

"Because he's walking up behind you right now, and by the look on his face, he's here as the county sheriff and not as your husband, former or otherwise."

# CHAPTER ELEVEN

"I need to talk to you, Carolina." Billy Sanchez approached her in the parking lot. If the desert was known for its hot days and cooler nights, seeing her former husband sent Carolina back to the frigid northern country of Wyoming. She turned to face him with ice running through her veins.

How dare he insist upon seeing her? How dare he be the sheriff of their hometown? "What is it, Billy?" Carolina asked. "I just got back to town, and I'm quite busy."

"It's about the murder," Billy said. She guessed he was off duty by the casual blue jeans and button-down shirt he wore, although he was still clearly armed. "I need to know if there is anything you can tell me about what happened here earlier between the woman we have in custody and her employees."

"I've already shared everything I know," Carolina said. "Jocelyn seems like a vile woman anyway. I wouldn't want to work for her if my life depended on it."

"She isn't always as bad as she comes off," Billy said.

Carolina thought she read something in his eyes. "Seriously? You and the caterer?"

"No, nothing like that," he said, but his face had turned scarlet red.

Carolina forced herself to refrain from saying what was on her mind. "You might want to head over to Chefs and More, the restaurant store in the city."

"Why would I travel almost an hour away?" Billy asked.

"Because the missing assistant you're looking for works there," Carolina said. "I just spoke with her."

"You what?" Billy's eyes widened, and his face turned an even deeper red, a characteristic Carolina remembered from their marriage that meant he was fuming mad. "You spoke with the missing woman, and you only now decided to share that with me? You're unbelievable." He rushed back to his pickup truck and said something into a radio receiver before coming back over to her.

"I was going to tell you as soon as I got to town, but I got here and was a little sidetracked by Levi and some guy he met with. I didn't know what they were up to."

"So, you had an argument with your employee instead of calling the police to let them know you were aware of the whereabouts of a missing woman." Billy shook his head again. "What did she say to you?"

Carolina sighed and leaned against her car. "Esme said Jocelyn and Paul had a disagreement about who was in charge of the company. Paul invested his own money in the catering business, and he liked to remind her of that," she said.

"She told you all of this?" Billy asked. "Freely, or did you go there begging for information?"

"What?" Carolina snapped. "I know you aren't trying to say that I somehow knew she'd be there, so I drove that far just to get involved in your investigation. Believe it or not, Billy, I have better things to do than continue to one-up you. I'm pretty good at that without any police matters at hand. Esme freely told me all of that while she helped me buy a new warming table and other things for the catering business we're starting."

Billy laughed and shook his head. "You know, it is a little odd that you just swooped into town and decided to start a catering service yourself. And on the very same day, a member of the competition just happens to wind up dead."

"You can ask Uncle Toad and Marissa and even Levi how that came about," Carolina shouted. "If that's not good enough for you, ask the mayor himself. While you're at it, you can also ask them where I've been all day."

Billy shook his head at her. "I have to go. Please try not to do anything else to set this investigation back. Otherwise, I might be forced to arrest you for obstruction of justice." He slammed the pickup door shut and sped off out of the parking lot.

Levi walked up behind her. "Well, there's no issue at all between you and the sheriff now, is there?" he said. Carolina had almost forgotten that he was still there, and the sound of his voice startled her. "Whoa, you don't have to be so jumpy, lady."

"It's just been a very, very long day, and tomorrow doesn't look a whole lot better."

"At least you're not sitting in jail tonight," Levi said.

"What is it about everyone reminding me of that?" Carolina asked.

"I don't know." Levi shrugged. "Maybe you just need to count your blessings."

Carolina nodded. "Maybe I should," she said. "For now, I'm going back to my room for a good night's rest."

"Okay, then," Levi said. "I suppose I'll lock up here."

Carolina sighed. She felt the sudden urge to roll her eyes. "Levi, do you need more help here tonight before I leave?"

"Yeah," Levi said. "You can help me arrange everything in the storage room before you go. Since you're the one who brought the stuff here and all."

"You're right." Carolina headed back inside and worked alongside Levi for an hour. They moved boxes and arranged the storage space to accommodate the catering supplies.

"Josiah is going to let me know about a van," Levi said when they were finished. "He has a line on a really good deal."

Carolina sighed. "Levi, be straight with me," she said. "Where is he going to get a good deal on a van? We can't afford to mess with anything that might be outside of the law. Even a little bit."

Levi fixed his eyes on her for a long moment. "You're unbelievable," he said at last, shaking his head at her. "Josiah runs a mission in Santa Fe."

"A mission? What kind of a mission?" she asked.

"The kind that feeds homeless people and helps get them off the street," Levi said. "He's dedicated his life to helping others, and he's a friend of your uncle's. That's how I know him." Just like Billy before him, Levi sauntered across the parking lot to this own vehicle and left without another word to her.

## CHAPTER TWELVE

It was late when Carolina arrived back at the Sycamore Ridge Inn. She threw her clothes off and stepped into a hot shower, hoping to forget most of the day. When the cold water began to replace the hot, she stepped out, wrapped her hair in a towel, and dressed for bed. In the morning, she would check out for the last time and head to the bank before she drove just outside of town.

She pulled one of her last couple outfits from her bag and sighed, knowing she'd have to visit the laundromat soon. So much needed to be done in the coming days, but her priority was the event on Saturday. She closed her eyes and leaned against the headboard on the motel room bed.

Esme's face filled her mind when she slipped off

to sleep a short time later. She followed her around the restaurant supply store and listened to her tales of woe, many a result of Carolina's active imagination, about the evil Jocelyn. In her dream, Jocelyn appeared in the store, red faced and spewing angry words. She sat upright when the woman got into her car and drove it at break-neck speed toward the store.

Carolina shook her head and stood up suddenly. Her neck muscles ached from the position she had slept in against the back of the bed. She walked to the window and peered out into the night, staring into the distant sky, still a little more pink and orange than dark and inky black. She missed the mountains that surrounded her in Wyoming, but there was something about the desert at night that made her spirit restless and eager for change.

She turned back to the sparse room. Her belongings were few. The old Airstream she had just agreed to purchase seemed like a good choice for her present state. Anything and everything of value she had in Jackson Hole was sold before she left, down to the very outfit she wore on her last night there. There was something about purging her possessions that felt like a baptism, a rite needed to leave behind her old life and to return to her even older one.

One thing she had not left behind was her nearly

new laptop computer. She picked up the card on the small entertainment center with the motel's Wi-Fi password and instructions and balanced the laptop on her knees. She opened the lid and entered the password, then waited while the computer connected to the super-slow internet. After a brief check of her social media accounts, Carolina started to shut the lid again, but paused when she thought of Marissa. She wondered if her cousin had mentioned anything about the catering business, and what the public might have thought of it.

Marissa's profile page was filled with numerous photos of baby things. She had links to rustic-looking cribs and gauzy white blankets. Carolina smiled and scrolled through the posts. She followed one of the links to a baby registry and purchased a gender-neutral layette to be delivered in a few days.

Marissa's last post was not a mention of the Hart Family Restaurant's new catering endeavors, but a link to a small news story about the death of Paul Wayver. Carolina followed the link and read through the story. Precious few details were included. Where his body was found and what time of day were among them, along with a brief mention of Jocelyn's arrest. There was no mention of the details of his death. Carolina found herself grateful for it.

Now fully awake, Carolina decided to look a little harder into the catering business. She searched online for more information about Jocelyn's catering firm, Nouvelle Chic. She found the website quickly.

"Someone spent a lot of money on this site," Carolina said aloud. She knew enough about building sites from her years in the marketing business that the website was essential to a business like hers. Jocelyn had spared no expense.

Carolina perused the few reviews included on the site. Most of them praised her sophisticated fare and presentation. She searched for the names of the business owners or individuals who had written the reviews but found nothing.

With another tab open, Carolina searched for more reviews of Nouvelle Chic. Three websites listed dozens, some as glowing as the reviews on the firm's website, but the rest were less than positive. This time, Carolina recognized the names of several local businesses and organizations.

Jocelyn clearly had her admirers, but she was not a good fit for everyone around Sycamore Ridge. Some of the reviewers complained of the ultra-fancy repast, the high cost, and the lack of enough food for a crowd. Carolina shrugged. Jocelyn was clearly an accomplished chef of a very particular niche, but her niche wasn't for everyone, it seemed. She smiled, thinking that it was clear that a second catering option was warranted, and there was no way Jocelyn was going to run her out of town.

Aside from the reviews, Carolina found nothing else of significance online about the company or the owner. Nothing that led to a specific person who would want to have killed Paul, anyway.

Curious, she turned to a quick search of Esme Feldman and Paul Wayver. Aside from the brief newspaper article mentioning Paul's unfortunate death, she found very little else about either one of Jocelyn's assistants that might have pointed toward them having anything to do with each other outside of the business. If Esme had something to do with Paul's death, she wasn't going to learn about it online.

Carolina's eyes ached from staring at the screen after the long day she had endured. She closed the computer and set it aside, then snuggled down in the bed and tried to get what sleep she could. Most of the night was spent tossing and turning or gazing out the window at the star-covered sky. She slept very little and around seven in the morning, she gave up for good and decided that it was time to face the day.

She was packed and ready to check out of the motel by nine. Carolina skipped the complimentary breakfast in the lobby and headed out to her car with her things. She drove around town for a few minutes searching for a bank that was already open for business and willing to write her a cashier's check without having an account there. After a short drive through the downtown area and past the Hart Family Restaurant, she found herself on the east side of town.

Mayor Martinez had said that the town of Sycamore Ridge was building up on the east side but had not told her the entire truth. Everything was already built. Carolina drove a mile down a road that had been sparsely populated when she'd left for Jackson Hole. In that short stretch of road, she counted seven fast food places, a shopping center, three big box retail stores and a church. She passed by a wooden sign that read "Welcome to East Sycamore Ridge," though it looked more ornamental than official.

She found an open bank and went inside. In a few short minutes, she paid a fee and had a cashier's check for the Lopez family and the paperwork to transfer the rest of her funds from her bank in Wyoming. She cringed slightly when she read the remaining balance on the receipt as she slowly walked to her car.

# CHAPTER THIRTEEN

"I can't thank you enough for this," Herman Lopez said. He folded the cashier's check over once and placed it into his shirt pocket.

"Where can I get the feed for the chickens?" Carolina asked. She was shocked to see so many hens flocking to the fence when she walked by.

"There's a feed store on the east side of town, but I prefer to run by the grain elevator a few miles from here. I'll write down directions if you're interested."

Carolina nodded. "Please, I have a feeling East Sycamore Ridge is not going to be my favorite place to go."

Herman returned to his own house and left Carolina alone to explore the interior of her Airstream. She pushed the key into the lock and opened the door. She set her suitcase and her extra bag down on the small sofa in the living area, then slid into the small dinette. It was a cozy fit, but not too tight. With her open palm, she felt the material and smiled. The upholstery was in good repair.

After another minute or two at the table, Carolina moved to the back of the trailer. She was pleased to see the bedroom more up close this time. The place was small, there was no doubt, but in reality, there wasn't much more she would need.

The best part was her proximity to the restaurant. She locked up the house and headed back to her car. Although she'd arrived in just under five minutes, Carolina had spent the short car ride reviewing the past few days of her life. Her week began with a last hurrah at her favorite watering hole in Wyoming and ended with a new home of her own and a new business venture.

The murder of her competition's chief assistant was another wrinkle altogether.

As she backed out of her driveway, she stopped and looked back at her new, shiny home. This place was hers, her new happy place. Her safe haven. She smiled as she drove back to the restaurant.

"How is the new place?" Marissa asked when she walked inside.

"Mine." Carolina grinned. She squeezed her cousin's arm as she passed by.

"That's the best way to be," Marissa whispered to her.

"Good morning, Carolina Maria," Uncle Toad said when she made her way into the back. "Levi here tells me that the two of you made a very wise purchase last night."

"Oh, did he?" Carolina asked. "Levi? Is everything settled with Josiah and the van?"

"We just have to pick it up this afternoon," Levi said. "Along with two grand for the down payment." His whispered words went only as far as her ears. Carolina looked over at her uncle, who was busy behind the grill.

"Okay," Carolina whispered back. "I can come up with the cash this afternoon." She was not thrilled about the thought of dipping further into her savings but didn't see much of a choice.

"Cash? Really?" Levi appeared surprised. "You don't have to go to the bank and get a loan?"

"I have some money," she said. "I used a bunch of it to buy a place this morning, but I still have some left."

Levi smiled at her, leaving her to wonder why. She didn't have too much time to think. Uncle Toad placed a plate on the pass-through window and turned around with a concerned face. "The sheriff is here to see you again," he said to Carolina.

"Last night and this morning." Levi clucked his tongue at her. "Sounds like unfinished business to me."

Carolina ignored him and headed straight to the front.

"Sheriff Sanchez," she said when she walked up to the booth where he was waiting. "Uncle Toad said that you needed to speak to me?"

"I need to ask you some more questions about your interaction with Esme yesterday," he said. He stared down at the table as he spoke. "I need for you to tell me the truth, the entire truth."

Carolina slid into the seat across from him. "I have never done anything but tell you the truth, Billy. Why would you think anything different?"

"Because I spoke to Esme, and she had a completely different recollection of your interaction with her," he said.

"What did she tell you?" Carolina asked.

"I really don't want to get into everything she had to say, but she made it sound as if you were the one really pushing for Jocelyn's arrest," Billy said. "She said that you were trying to get her to say that she had seen a fight between Jocelyn and Paul yesterday morning."

"That never happened," Carolina said. She could feel her throat tighten at his words. Why would a complete stranger say that about her?

"I need for you to be real straight with me here," Billy said. He looked up at her finally. "Someone could take a look at you coming into town hoping to start a catering business and believe that you decided to take advantage of a situation when it presented itself."

"Are you seriously suggesting that I rode into town with the desire to usurp a catering business I had never heard of and then had the presence of mind to predict that Jocelyn was going to murder her assistant?" Carolina said. "You can't actually buy all of that!"

"You're saying that's not what happened?" Billy asked her.

"I'm saying that the version of events I gave you last night is the truth," she said. "If you need more proof, go ask around the restaurant supply store again. I bet you could even find our interaction on video tape."

"Last chance to change your story, Carolina," Billy said. "You're willing to swear by the statements you made about your conversation with Esme?"

"In court, on a Bible, in front of a judge and jury." Carolina stood up, leaned over the table, and stared him right in the eyes.

"Alright," Billy said. "I had to ask. We've decided to release Jocelyn from custody. She has an alibi that checks out."

"That's good," Carolina said boldly. "If she is innocent, she shouldn't be in jail."

"You wouldn't have tried to put her there just to make yourself a little less competition? Maybe tried to frame her in some way?"

Carolina stood upright and planted both hands firmly on her hips. "Absolutely not, Sheriff," she said. "If you took the time to really check into her business, you would see that her approach to food is far different from what you see here on my family's menu," she said. "We aren't in competition."

"Look, I'm just doing my job here," Billy said. He stood up to leave. "If you think of anything else, you will reach out and let me know." With that, he replaced his hat on his head and sauntered out the door to his waiting squad car.

Carolina watched him for a second, then turned to head back to the kitchen. She stopped midstep and turned back to the windows. "I know who did it!" she shouted.

"What are you talking about?" Levi called to her.

"I'll be right back." She sprinted toward the door.

"Billy, wait!" Carolina raised her arms over her head when she ran outside. He had already backed his car out of the parking spot. She ran around to the side, still waving her arms.

"What is it?" he asked when he rolled down the window.

"I just thought of something," she said, trying to catch her breath. "When you were busy suggesting that I framed Jocelyn for some absurd reason, it occurred to me that Esme may have done that exact thing."

"What do you mean by that?" Billy asked.

"Well, during the original meeting when we took over the catering event, Paul said he'd do anything to make sure that the mayor was gone after for breach of contract. Esme tried to talk him out of it, but he wasn't having it."

"I assume there's more to your story?" Billy raised a brow.

Carolina nodded. "When I went to the restaurant supply store, Esme helped me find all the things I was looking for. She also said she'd get a commission."

"And? That's pretty common in a job like that, isn't it?"

"Maybe so, but she also said she had to get a part-time job there because her hours with Jocelyn were unpredictable. To me, that means she was short on cash. What if she stopped Paul from doing anything about it by running him off the road?"

"In order to get a few dollars in commission?" Billy huffed. "That's ridiculous."

"Not if she was tired of dealing with Jocelyn, barely getting any hours, and over listening to her and Paul argue all the time. Plus, it was way more than a few dollars, I'm sure. I spent thousands, and she knew I'd be coming back for more. It might not have been a long-term answer, but it would sure help her out in the now. Paul even said something about her wanting work so she could pay for her oversized house."

"So, you think she tried to frame Jocelyn, but how?"

"Well, during that same meeting, Jocelyn was furious and took off out of the restaurant, but not before she ordered Esme to get her things. Esme also said at the restaurant supply store that she had access to all of Jocelyn's information. What if one of those things Esme took was Jocelyn's phone? She could have sent the text to Paul, right?"

Billy sighed hard. "Did you see her take the phone?"

Carolina gripped the side of the car. She leaned in the passenger window and exhaled. "No, but…"

"Carolina."

"Wait! We have cameras!"

Billy picked up the radio receiver in his car and mumbled a few words into it. He replaced it on the hook and glared at Carolina. "Show me."

She raced inside and breezed past everyone on her way to the office. She pressed a few buttons on the old camera system and hoped for the best. Moments later, there was proof that Esme picked up Jocelyn's cell phone. It wasn't going to be enough, but it was sure going to help.

# CHAPTER FOURTEEN

Carolina woke early Saturday morning and headed into the Hart Family Restaurant. She was already dressed in her most comfortable jeans and a simple, short-sleeved shirt. She slipped her feet into her best running shoes. Few chances would come to her today to be off her feet.

She arrived at the restaurant around the same time Marissa opened the front doors to customers. Levi and Uncle Toad switched off at the grill while the other one chopped steak and vegetables for the cooler. Carolina tied an apron around her middle and went to work running between helping Marissa in the front and the guys in the back.

Between the breakfast and lunch rushes, she took a seat in the dining room. The day's menus and schedules were laid out on the table in front of her. She took long, deep breaths as she studied them and wondered if she was going to be able to pull everything together for her first catering gig.

Before lunch, more eager faces appeared at the Hart Family Restaurant. Danny Lopez, Marissa's husband, arrived and donned an apron, as did a couple of her friends. Herman and Margie, Danny's parents and Carolina's new next-door neighbors, did the same.

When the lunch rush was over, Levi and Uncle Toad began grilling meat and filling the warming table that had arrived the day before. Despite everything, the table had arrived in the nick of time and worked beautifully.

Around two, Carolina took to the kitchen herself. Armed with one of the large metal bowls she had purchased at the restaurant supply store, she carefully began to measure out flour while she stood at the prep table, typically run by Levi. She could feel his eyes on her as she mixed in the salt, warm water, eggs, and melted butter for the empanadas.

When the dough was ready, she returned to the storage room and set it in the cooler to chill for an hour. Next, she gathered the seasonings together, some she had purchased at the restaurant supply store just for the empanadas. She included cumin, salt and pepper, smoked paprika, cayenne, thyme, and oregano.

Carolina reluctantly took over part of her uncle's grill. She was nervous as she chopped and seasoned the beef. She added diced onions, green peppers, green chiles, and jalapeños to the beef mixture. As she worked, she made a list of the seasonings she used. The list was the start of her shopping list for the next run to the city.

While the meat sizzled, Carolina returned to the cooler for the dough. She began the process of rolling out the pastry in round circles, then removed the meat and vegetables from the grill. She added tomato sauce to the mixture in a large bowl and began putting the empanadas together. The inside of the Hart Family Restaurant smelled like magic to her as she and the rest of the staff worked quietly together to prepare to feed two hundred people in just a matter of hours.

As she worked, Carolina was grateful for the busy work the empanadas required. Her hands moved faster than the worry in her head, most of the time anyway. She tried to keep the anxiety building in her mind to a dull roar. As she worked, she told herself the dinner would either work out, or it wouldn't.

There was so much riding on the thought that it

would. She could feel her mother's hands guiding her own as she shaped the dough and then impressed fork tines to seal each empanada after she assembled it. After the edges were crimped together, Carolina deep fried the empanadas in small batches then transferred them to the warming table for safekeeping while everyone else began to load the van.

When the van was full, Levi slid behind the wheel, and Uncle Toad got into the passenger seat. They headed directly for the community center. Carolina followed with Marissa in the car with her while her husband, friends, and his parents drove behind them. They arrived just after four and began removing the food from the van. While Uncle Toad and Levi set up in the large kitchen, Marissa and Carolina placed white linen tablecloths on each of the tables and assembled the chairs.

Under Uncle Toad's instructions, Danny and his parents worked to set up the food stations. Margie Lopez took over part of the kitchen to create her famous flan and help with chopping vegetables for the fajita station. Carolina put together her mother's cilantro-lime dipping sauce for the empanadas and other appetizers, then helped her uncle with the queso.

Just after six, the mayor arrived and toured the

kitchen. Carolina was sure she witnessed a look of intense relief on his face when he saw how things were going. Just before seven, the guests were seated, and the room buzzed with chatter. Carolina stood back in the kitchen and directed the others serving appetizers to each table. The mayor took his place in front of the podium and began his address.

After a few brief speeches, the dinner portion of the evening was in full swing. Levi manned the fajita station while Carolina, Marissa, and the others ensured each station remained fully stocked with ingredients from the kitchen.

Halfway through the dinner break, Carolina stepped outside of the kitchen for a moment to catch her breath. She rubbed the middle of her lower back and sighed. Her feet were killing her. She could scarcely imagine how Marissa was getting on.

"You're really pulling this off, aren't you?" Billy approached her. Carolina instantly stood up straight and felt herself on guard.

"I, um, well, we're doing this," she stammered. "Together. My family and me."

"The food is incredible." Billy smiled. He was dressed in a more formal version of his normal uniform. "Your restaurant always was my favorite place to eat."

Carolina softened slightly. The look in his eyes brought memories back to her from two decades before.

"I'm so grateful for my family right now," she said. "They really stepped up to help me."

"I can see that," Billy said. "Speaking of stepping up, your tip about Esme paid off. She confessed to the whole thing after I picked her up."

"She confessed?"

Billy nodded. "Your quick thinking prevented an innocent woman from going to prison," he said. "I don't know how you remembered such a small detail about your conversation, but that small detail solved a murder. Maybe you should join the police force."

"No, thank you," Carolina said. "That was always your dream."

"Too bad that dream didn't fit with yours," Billy said suddenly, then tipped his hat to her. He turned back to the large, central room where the ceremony was about to resume.

Carolina closed her eyes for a moment, then exhaled sharply. Now was not the time to question comments made by her former husband. She still had hours to go before she could consider the night a success. When she opened her eyes again, she was face to face with Jocelyn Hendricks. Her arms were folded over her chest, and her face held its typical sneer.

"I suppose you've done it," Jocelyn said. "Somehow you put together a large, three-course meal for this event. I suppose the rookie mistakes I see can be overlooked, given the fact that you have managed not to burn the building down on your first try. Who knew diner food would suffice for this crowd?"

"Good to see you, too, Jocelyn," Carolina said.

"Oh, it is good to see anybody right now," Jocelyn said. She dropped her arms to her side and slowly let her breath out. "I understand that I have you to thank for ultimately clearing my name, even if I had a solid alibi."

"I just told the sheriff the truth about what Esme said," Carolina said. "You don't owe me anything for that."

"Oh, I know I don't owe you anything." Jocelyn's face brightened. "Besides, I already paid that debt to you by allowing your little catering adventure to go on. In fact, I'm feeling so generous right now that I'm not going to shut you down completely after this night is over. I've decided that there is room for two of us in this town, Carolina."

"Well, thank you," she said with a shrug. "Our

menus are so different anyway. It isn't like we're going to run in the same circles, anyway."

"Oh, I already know that," Jocelyn said with a scoff. "You're all down-home cooking and comfort food, while my team is more for the sophisticated and tasteful crowd."

Carolina sighed. "As long as we have that straight," she said. "Now, if you will excuse me, I am needed in the kitchen."

"Before you go, let me give you two pieces of advice for free," Jocelyn said. "One, invest in better clothes for these events. As the owner of a catering company, you need to look the part, but be sure what you wear is also comfortable."

"Good to know," Carolina said. "And the other thing?"

Jocelyn grinned. She leaned in and whispered, "You better do your homework before the next gig comes up, because the competition is on. I will fight you every step of the way for each important catering contract I can in this town. Just because you saved me from prison doesn't mean I'm going to roll over and let you rob me of what I've built here."

"Duly noted," Carolina said. "And two things in return, Jocelyn."

"What two things could you possibly have to say to me?"

"Well, for one, you're welcome. Despite our differences, I wouldn't want to see you go to prison for something you didn't do," Carolina said. "And the other thing? Competition doesn't scare me a bit. Bring it on."

"Duly noted," Jocelyn smirked. She turned around with a knowing grin and headed back to the awards dinner. Carolina watched as she walked away, and decided she was right about one thing for sure. It was time to look the part of a professional caterer.

\*\*

**If you enjoyed High Steaks Murder, check out the next book in the series, Souped Up Murder, today!**

# AUTHOR'S NOTE

I'd love to hear your thoughts on my books, the storylines, and anything else that you'd like to comment on—reader feedback is very important to me. My contact information, along with some other helpful links, is listed on the next page. If you'd like to be on my list of "folks to contact" with updates, release and sales notifications, etc.... just shoot me an email and let me know. Thanks for reading!

Also...

... if you're looking for more great reads, Summer Prescott Books publishes several popular series by outstanding Cozy Mystery authors.

# CONTACT SUMMER PRESCOTT BOOKS PUBLISHING

Blog and Book Catalog: http://summerprescottbooks.com

Email: summer.prescott.cozies@gmail.com

And…be sure to check out the Summer Prescott Cozy Mysteries fan page and Summer Prescott Books Publishing Page on Facebook – let's be friends!

To sign up for our fun and exciting newsletter, which will give you opportunities to win prizes and swag, enter contests, and be the first to know about New Releases, click here: http://summerprescottbooks.com

Printed in Great Britain
by Amazon

45489981R00071